Published by Grandreams Books Ltd,
4 North Parade, Bath, BA1 1LF, UK.

Grandreams Books Inc.,
360 Hurst Street, Linden, NJ 07036 USA
Printed in China.

50
BEDTIME
STORIES

Written by Anne McKie
Illustrated by Ken McKie

CONTENTS

Lucky Bear

One morning the postman brought Lindy a letter. It was an invitation to a party.

Her mother read it out to her, "Please come to a party from three-thirty until six o'clock, and bring your teddy bear too..."

Now Lindy's Aunt Meg had given her a new tiny teddy bear that very morning – she had brought it back from her holiday.

"I think I'll take my new bear," smiled Lindy, "he'll enjoy meeting all the other bears."

"He's so new, you haven't given him a name," said Mum. "Careful you don't lose him, he's so small!"

But Lindy was so excited about the birthday party and so busy getting ready, she forgot about her new teddy's name.

That afternoon, as soon as the clock struck three, Lindy put the tiny teddy into her coat pocket and set off with Mum to the party.

All the children had remembered to bring a bear and everyone had a great time. They played Pass the Parcel, Blind Man's Bluff and lots of other party games. Everybody enjoyed the party food as well – lots of delicious snacks. And they had the biggest birthday cake anybody had ever seen! Everybody had lots of fun... and I'm sure the bears enjoyed it too!

At six o'clock it was time to go home. The boys and girls gathered up their bears and were each given a lucky bag full of sweets. But poor Lindy couldn't find her little teddy bear anywhere!

Her mum and the other parents searched everywhere, behind cushions, under chairs, in cupboards and even in the rubbish bag!

"I'm afraid we'll have to go home without your little teddy bear," said Mum. "We'll have another look tomorrow."

So Lindy said, "goodbye and thank you," looking very sad indeed.

"Don't forget your lucky bag!" called the lady who had held the party.

That night Lindy went to bed feeling very unhappy.

"Poor little teddy," she sniffed, very close to tears. "I wonder where he is at this very moment?"

"I think I know!" grinned her mother, as she opened the lucky bag from the party. "Take a look inside!"

Lindy peeped inside the bag, and there was the tiny teddy – he'd never been lost at all.

"I think I'll call him LUCKY!" grinned Lindy, and they both fell fast asleep!

Mr Wolf in a Spin

Crafty Mr Wolf was always trying to catch the three little pigs so he could gobble them up!

But this didn't worry those three little pigs one bit, for they were far too clever for that wicked wolf!

On this particular morning, Mr Wolf had spent several hours plotting and planning how to trap the three little pigs.

All of a sudden he leapt up from the table, threw all his papers up into the air, and began to dance round and round the room in glee.

"I've thought of the perfect plan!" cried a very excited Mr Wolf. "This time I shall catch those three plump little pigs once and for all!" He then spun round and round, and began to feel very dizzy.

"Oh dear me!" gasped Mr Wolf as he reached for his chair. "I always feel dizzy if I turn round more than once!"

Now, can you see who is looking through Mr Wolf's window and listening to his every word?

As you can imagine, it wasn't very long before those three clever little pigs thought of a perfect plan of their own. It made them squeal with laughter so loudly they ran home as fast as they could – just in case that wicked Mr Wolf heard them.

As soon as they were safe inside their house, the three little pigs took all the money from their piggy banks and emptied the coins into a small bag. Then they rushed back to Mr Wolf's house and knocked on his front door. They couldn't wait for him to answer the door so they could put their plan into action.

"Good afternoon, Mr Wolf," said the three little pigs all at once. "We would like you to come to the fair with us and help spend all this money!"

Mr Wolf couldn't believe his ears and, of course, he agreed at once.

When they arrived at the fair, the three little pigs bought Mr Wolf a big bag of sweets, four large ice-creams, a huge bucket of toffee-flavoured popcorn and a very sticky lolly. Suddenly Mr Wolf spied a crowd of woodland folk sitting comfortably in some enormous tea cups.

"I'd like to have a rest for a while and enjoy my lolly," Mr Fox yawned. "I feel quite tired after spending so much of your money!" Mr Wolf grinned as he stepped inside an empty tea cup.

The three little pigs' plan was working perfectly! Then, without any warning at all, those giant tea cups began to spin round and round. The quicker the cups spun round, the more the woodland folk shrieked with delight.

"Isn't this fun?" yelled the three little pigs, as their tea cup whizzed round faster and faster.

"Help! Help!" screamed poor Mr Wolf, his face turning bright green. "Please stop this tea cup, I want to get off!"

At long last the tea-cup ride came to an end. The three cheeky little pigs helped a very dizzy Mr Wolf out of his cup, and then pushed him all the way home in a wheelbarrow.

"We could take you to the fair again if you have no plans for tomorrow," said one little pig, giggling.

"I don't think I'll be making any more plans for a very long time!" gasped the wolf, as he collapsed in a heap into his favourite armchair.

The Pull-Along Duck

The little Pull-Along Duck had lived in his toy box ever since he could remember.

"I have never been in a pond or a stream," he said with a tear in his eye. "I don't even know if I can swim!"

"All ducks can swim," said his friend the Blue Monkey, kindly. "I'm sure if you went into the water you would be one of the best swimmers around!"

Then one night the Pull-Along Duck was left outside in the garden quite by mistake. During the night there was a great thunderstorm. It rained so hard, the lawn was soon under water.

To his great surprise, the Pull-Along Duck floated across the garden and straight into the fish pond. Suddenly he began to swim round and round. The little wooden duck was delighted.

He had such fun – and he was so happy to find that he could swim just like any other duck.

The next morning, a little girl found him. She dried him with a towel ever so carefully, and then popped him back in the toy box.

When the little Blue Monkey heard all about the Pull-Along Duck's adventure, he promised that every so often he would take him out to the garden, so he could swim round and round the fish pond.

Gordon's New Caravan

Gordon the gorilla was very strong. He could bend iron bars with ease, lift the heaviest of weights high above his head, and he could even pull a car... with his TEETH!

It was holiday time and the weather was hot and sunny, so Gordon decided to go camping. He booked into a camp site and pitched his brand new tent. But when poor Gordon tried to get inside it, he discovered his tent was much too small... or he was far too big!

"You will never fit into a tent, Gordon!" a helpful little boy scout told him. "I think you should try a caravan."

So off went young Gordon to the nearest town.

"They're just like houses on wheels!" grinned Gordon.

So he bought the biggest caravan he could find, and took it back to the camp site.

The helpful little boy scout was waiting for him at the gates.

"Gordon," said the helpful little boy, "you tow a caravan with a car... NOT WITH YOURSELF!"

Mum's Long Weekend

An old school friend had asked Mum to go and stay with her for a weekend.

"It will be a long weekend," said Mum. "Can you four manage without me?"

"Certainly," said Dad, with a weak smile. "You go off and enjoy yourself."

So off went Mum on her long weekend. Her little girls, Dolly, Molly and Holly, had agreed to keep their rooms tidy and do the dusting while Dad did the rest of the housework.

First he vacuumed the carpets, which took no time at all. Then he did the washing, which was really quite easy. Next came the ironing, which took more time than Dad had imagined. Dolly, Molly and Holly were impressed!

The long weekend passed very quickly, and on the morning that Mum was due back, Dad got up early to bake her a cake. Now making a cake was taking a lot longer than Dad had planned.

"I meant to go out and buy your mother a big bunch of pretty flowers to welcome her home," said Dad as he gazed at his baking.

"Don't worry!" called Dolly, Molly and Holly, and they rushed out into the garden to pick the brightest flowers they could find.

At last Mum returned, and on the table was a cake and a vase of fresh flowers.

"What a splendid cake and such unusual flowers!" cried Mum, and she glanced at Dad.

Now Dad had been so busy with the cake, he hadn't noticed that Dolly, Molly

and Holly had picked all the flowers from his prize beans.

"Let's all have some of my cake," said Dad. "Then I'll go out to the garden and plant some more beans!"

Fizzy Grizzly's Gift

Fizzy Grizzly's grandma had hurt her back, so she had to stay indoors for a little while.

"My gran loves honey buns," Fizzy Grizzly suddenly remembered. "I shall bake some straight away and take them over to her house this very afternoon!"

When Fizzy Grizzly's honey buns came out of the oven, they were absolutely perfect. They were the perfect colour and the perfect shape... and they smelt delicious!

As he looked at the baking tray, groaning with the weight of the honey buns, Fizzy Grizzly could feel his mouth watering. Honey buns were his favourite things in the whole world!

"I must not eat any!" said Fizzy Grizzly, popping them into a basket as soon as they were cool.

Half-way to Gran's house he sat down for a rest under a tree in the woods. He sneaked a peek inside his basket and sniffed.

"These honey buns smell simply delicious," sighed Fizzy Grizzly, "I'll just try one!"

Now bears love honey, and they especially love honey buns. So before Fizzy Grizzly could stop himself, he'd eaten the lot!

"Whatever shall I do?" cried Fizzy Grizzly. "I've been a really greedy bear, there's not a single honey bun left."

Fizzy looked around the wood, most disappointed with himself. Then, suddenly, he spotted some juicy wild strawberries, and hanging right above his head were bunches of shiny black cherries. As quickly as he could, Fizzy Grizzly filled up his basket.

Fizzy's grandma was delighted with all the fresh cherries and strawberries that Fizzy had brought her.

"Everyone has been ever so kind," she said, "but they have all brought me honey cakes and honey buns. You will have to help me eat them all up Fizzy dear!"

It's a Parade!

Farmer William's ducks loved to march round and round the duck pond, quacking at the tops of their voices. They thought it sounded very musical, but no-one else in the farmyard agreed.

Now sly Mr Fox would often hide behind a big willow tree and watch the ducks quacking and marching.

He would smack his lips loudly and smile to himself, for he was always dreaming of roast duck for his dinner!

"Those ducks are marching round and round again," he sniggered. "I think I'll join in and show them how to do it properly," and he strode over to the duck pond.

"You're doing it all wrong," shouted Mr Fox to the little ducks. "I'll show you how to march in time. Just follow me everyone!"

So the wily Mr Fox set off towards his house with all the ducks marching alongside him. Left, right! Left, right!

He marched the ducks down the lane, across the field and right up to his gate.

Mr Fox was really enjoying this, shouting orders and swinging his arms. Left, right! Left, right!

Now Mr Fox was so busy giving orders and thinking of all the juicy roast duck he would soon have for dinner, that he didn't even notice the ducks had circled round and were heading back towards the farmyard. He just followed them shouting,

"Ducks, pick up your feet. Left, right! Left, right!"

The little ducks turned swiftly into the farm gate and marched through the farmyard straight into the duck pond. Quite happily, they floated gently across the water.

Mr Fox, on the other hand, did not! He strode straight into the pond and sunk into the cold muddy water. What a shock for sly Mr Fox! As he struggled to the surface, coughing and spluttering and covered in slimy green duck-weed, he heard the ducks quacking loudly.

"No roast dinner for you today, Mr Fox. Fooled you, didn't we?"

"Aaargh," moaned Mr Fox, "I'll never have roast duck for my dinner at this rate!"

Danny's Tip-Up Trucks

One fine day in spring, Danny took his pull-along train outside. He filled his trucks with the smallest toys and took them out for a ride.

A few of the small toys pulled faces at the bigger ones left behind.

"You're far too big to fit!" yelled the clockwork penguin, rather rudely to the china doll. "So inside you stay!"

The big toys felt very disappointed. They watched glumly as the small toys set off on their adventure.

Now Danny wasn't too careful when he took his pull-along train outside, and when he ran across the lawn and down the steps, the small toys were tipped out one by one!

Some of them toppled over and bumped their heads, and the others were tossed out all over the lawn. There they stayed until bedtime when Danny's mother came out, picked them up and took them back indoors.

"Didn't you enjoy your ride in the pull-along train?" asked the china doll when she saw the small toys covered in grass and looking rather battered.

"Not one little bit! Next time you can go for a trip in Danny's pull-along train," said the penguin, "and I'm sorry I was so rude to you!"

"Don't worry," smiled the china doll. "We are big enough to sit on top of the trucks and not fall off."

So on the next fine day, the big toys had a great ride on the pull-along train, while the small toys stayed indoors and played quietly!

Barnaby and Brandy Go Camping

Barnaby Bear felt like having a weekend away. "I deserve a rest!" he said aloud. "I think I shall go camping in the woods at the bottom of Smokey Mountain."

"May I come too?" asked Brandy Bear, who had been sitting behind the fence, listening.

"Sure you can!" said Barnaby. "Be quick and pack your bag before I change my mind!" and he gave a big gruff laugh, just like bears do!

It wasn't long before the two bears were ready. They set off across the valley towards the woods at the bottom of Smokey Mountain, with Barnaby striding straight ahead and young Brandy struggling behind him.

Somehow Brandy's rucksack looks bigger than him. No wonder he keeps falling over!

When Barnaby Bear looked back, he found that young Brandy Bear was a long way behind.

"Whatever have you packed in that rucksack of yours?" shouted Barnaby.

"Only things that will come in useful!" gasped young Brandy, quite out of breath.

So Barnaby went over and picked up the heavy rucksack and gave Brandy his lighter one to carry.

At last the two bears reached the woods at the bottom of Smokey Mountain, and when Barnaby emptied Brandy's rucksack, what do you think he found?

Lots and lots of LOGS for their fire! Have you forgotten you're in the woods, Brandy? All around are... lots and lots of LOGS! You are a silly bear Brandy!

Aunt Chloe's Green Armchair

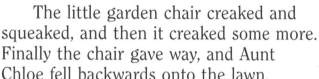

It was a very hot afternoon, far too hot to run about and play. So Janey and Josh were sitting under the shady garden umbrella doing nothing at all, and Dad was working hard clipping the hedge.

"Children, come and help me carry out some chairs and the table. Your Aunt Chloe is coming to tea this afternoon!" called Mum.

"Oh no, not Aunt Chloe," Janey and Josh muttered.

Now when Aunt Chloe came to tea everybody, even Dad, had to be on their very best behaviour.

"Coo-ee!" called a shrill voice from behind the hedge. It was Aunt Chloe; she gave Dad quite a shock.

"Goodness me, she's here already," whispered Mum. "Quick Janey, help me with the food! Josh, put out a chair for Aunt Chloe!"

"What scrumptious-looking trifle," said Aunt Chloe. Then she helped herself to a huge bowlful, and sat down with an enormous flop.

The little garden chair creaked and squeaked, and then it creaked some more. Finally the chair gave way, and Aunt Chloe fell backwards onto the lawn.

"Get me another chair while I cut myself a piece of that delicious-looking chocolate cake!" she called to Josh, as she scrambled to her feet and looked at what other gooey desserts were awaiting her on the table.

But as she sat down with a flop, the bottom fell out of the poor little picnic chair, and Aunt Chloe was on the ground once more!

Then it was Janey's turn to fetch a chair. She ran towards the house and got a cane chair from the porch.

Once again Aunt Chloe tried to take her seat. But when she flopped down on it, while reaching for a plate of cream buns, the legs of the chair snapped off one by one, and she tipped backwards into the flowerbed!

Poor Dad! He was most concerned about the state of his flowers – now they were covered in cream and trifle!

At last Aunt Chloe stood up. She brushed the crumbs and cream from her dress and pointed at the hedge Dad was still clipping.

"That green armchair will do just fine for me!" she chuckled, and she went to sit down with the last slice of lemon meringue pie... because that was all that was left!

Osbert the Funniest Onion

Osbert Onion was fed up with all the other vegetables crying every time he came near.

"Don't worry about it, Osbert," laughed a friendly turnip as tears rolled down his face. "Onions make everybody cry!"

So there and then Osbert decided to do something about it.

He rushed out to the shops and bought a brightly coloured clown's outfit and the biggest joke book he could find. All the vegetables crowded round when they saw Osbert come back, dressed as a clown. And when he told jokes from his big joke book, they all laughed and laughed. The more jokes Osbert told, the more those vegetables laughed. In fact,

the vegetables laughed so much they started to cry!

When poor Osbert saw this, he stopped telling jokes at once.

"I'm making you all cry again!" he said, looking very glum indeed.

"Please keep on telling jokes!" the vegetables yelled. "You're the Funniest Onion in the World! You make us cry because we are happy, not because we are sad!"

26

Texas Grandpa's Letters

At breakfast one morning, Texas Grandpa asked his young grandson, Pete, to take a trip into town with him to collect his letters.

"Are you feeling fit and strong today, Pete?" asked Texas Grandpa.

"Sure!" grinned Pete. "How ever many letters have you to collect, Grandpa?"

"Not that many," said Texas Grandpa with a wink, "but we had better take my biggest pick-up!"

Now Texas Grandpa always had sacks full of letters and cards on his birthday, but that wasn't for another six weeks. Pete looked very puzzled...

Was Pete in for a surprise when they collected the letters!

"I'm going to have a new sign on the gates of my ranch," laughed Grandpa, "and we do everything BIGGER in TEXAS!"

A Dragon Made the Tea

Great-aunt Jenny decided to stay with some relatives for a few days. After she arrived, she offered to take her young nephew, Ted, on a picnic.

"I used to go up Rumble-Tum hill when I was a little girl about the same age as you!" said Great-aunt Jenny.

"Why do you call it Rumble-Tum hill?" asked little Ted, who was always rather curious.

"Let's climb it, then you will see," smiled Jenny.

When Ted and Great-aunt Jenny reached the top of Rumble-Tum hill, they laid a tablecloth on the grass and set out their picnic of sandwiches and cakes. Ted's mouth started watering at the sight of the cheese and cucumber sandwiches, his favourite, and the biggest chocolate cake he had ever seen!

"All we need now," said Ted, "is a pot of tea."

"Oh, bother!" sighed Jenny, "I've forgotten the matches to light the stove to make the tea."

All of a sudden there came a strange, loud, rumbling sound from inside the hill. It was as if the entire hill was shaking. Poor Ted started feeling quite nervous.

Then, suddenly, a mighty dragon popped up! With one great fiery breath, he lit the stove. Great-aunt Jenny, not the least surprised, promptly made the tea.

"Will you stay for a cup?" she asked the dragon politely, and the dragon agreed. Ted just looked on in complete and utter amazement. He had read about dragons in books, he had thought they were dangerous creatures, but this one seemed perfectly pleasant and well-mannered. The dragon finished his cup of tea, thanked Jenny, smiled a fiery smile at Ted, and disappeared up the hill.

"Now you know why I call it Rumble-Tum hill!" said Great-aunt Jenny, as she and Ted started walking back home.

Ted looked at her and nodded, "I think we should just tell everyone that we went on a picnic and met someone who made a lovely cup of tea!"

"Very wise, Ted!" said Great-aunt Jenny.

Grandpa Meadowsweet's Surprise Garden

Grandpa Meadowsweet had been in hospital. When he came home he had to stay indoors for quite a while.

"We could look after your garden, Grandpa, until you feel better!" said his grandchildren Poppy and Pete.

So the very next day the children got out all their garden tools and started work.

Weeks went by, and Poppy and Pete grew busier and busier. They found lots of different seeds in Grandpa Meadowsweet's greenhouse, so they planted every packet.

On warm afternoons Grandpa would take a walk round his garden with Mother holding his arm.

"My garden looks rather bare," said Grandpa with a sigh. "I wonder what the children are doing?"

"I've no idea," said Mother with a smile, "but they are very busy!"

At long last Grandpa Meadowsweet felt completely better, and on one of the brightest days of the summer, he strode out into his garden.

"Still nothing growing here!" he said, looking puzzled. But what a surprise he got when he peeped round the corner.

For behind his potting shed and next to the greenhouse, the children had been hard at work. They had planted his seeds everywhere! In his wheelbarrow, in watering cans and buckets, in pots and pans, even in an old chair. Everything was filled with flowers. It was so colourful and pretty – the garden looked so cheerful.

"Well done," smiled Grandpa Meadowsweet as he wiped a tear from his eye. "I couldn't have done it better myself!"

Jumbo Gets the Jitters

One sunny day Jumbo Jet was parked on the tarmac at the airport looking very glum indeed.

"Whatever is the matter?" asked one of the other aeroplanes. "It's a beautiful day, not a cloud in the sky, it's perfect for flying!"

Just then a great big tear rolled slowly down Jumbo Jet's cheek and splashed onto the tarmac.

"I'm so frightened of flying," he whispered, "it gives me the jitters!"

"What are the jitters?" asked a small helicopter who was listening in.

"When I get the jitters, it makes me feel wibbly, wobbly and shaky, and it gives me the hiccups!" Jumbo exclaimed, looking round nervously.

"Then you should not be flying at all!" said the small helicopter.

"But I'm a jet aeroplane!" said Jumbo, and he began to cry.

At that very moment a Very Important Pilot came striding across the runway, looking rather serious.

"I am sorry to have to tell you aeroplanes," he shouted in a loud voice, "that one of you is needed on the ground... and I'm afraid it means giving up flying!"

Jumbo Jet stopped crying at once and moved forward.

"I have a volunteer!" cried the Very Important Pilot. "How simply splendid!"

From then on, Jumbo became a training aeroplane. Pilots came far and wide to sit in Jumbo's cockpit and learn how to fly.

And as for Jumbo... he never has to leave the runway.

Baby Bett and the Plumber

Baby Bett Brown was playing with her little toy hammer on the kitchen floor.

"She's making rather a lot of noise for such a little girl!" exclaimed Dad.

"I don't think it's Baby Bett," said Mum with a frown. "I think it's the kitchen tap or the pipes that are making that awful banging noise!"

"Better send for the plumber," said Dad with a sigh, picking up the telephone.

At long last the plumber came, and after drinking several mugs of tea with lots of sugar, he opened his bag of tools. He took out his biggest hammer and gave the pipes under the sink a WHACK... and the problem was solved!

Mr Brown thought this deserved another mug of tea and some of Mrs Brown's jam tarts, and the plumber agreed.

Now Bett, who had been very quiet all this time, had been very busy! She liked the plumber's big hammer much better than hers. So she popped her toy one into his bag and kept the big hammer for herself. The plumber will be most surprised when he goes to his next job. And Mr and Mrs Brown may get quite a shock when they see what Bett is doing!

The Ants Take the Biscuit

One day the ants went to a picnic, even though they didn't have a proper invitation.

Quite by chance, the ants' little house was right next to the picnic basket.

The folks at the picnic dropped all sorts of delicious crumbs, tasty bits of cake and crumbly flakes of pastry.

Then, lucky for those little ants, someone dropped a whole chocolate biscuit right into their larder!

"Don't worry," said a voice from above as the folks packed away their picnic. "It's only a chocolate biscuit!"

"It may be only a chocolate biscuit to them," chuckled a tiny ant, "but it's a whole winter's food for us ants!"

Fly Away Home

I expect you all know and can say the rhyme:

Ladybird, ladybird,
Fly away home,
Your house is on fire,
Your children are gone.

Now you can imagine how fed up Laura Ladybird felt when everyone said it to her at least twenty times a day!
"I'm not a bit worried if my house catches fire, and I know my children are quite safe," said Laura with a big grin, "because my husband Larry Ladybird is a FIREMAN!"

Match the Pairs

The weather was warm and dry and the wind was blowing fluffy white clouds across a clear blue sky.

"What a perfect day!" said Cordelia the centipede as she searched through her tiny house for a long length of string.

"It's perfect for kite-flying!" said her friend Willie the worm as he popped his head out from his hole in the ground.

"I'm sure it is," replied Cordelia, "but I've no time to go kite-flying today!" and she went on busily looking for her string.

"It's not the most perfect day for repairing my web," grumbled Sam the spider, as the wind blew his hat high in the air.

"But it's simply perfect for washing all my socks!" giggled Cordelia, as she found her string at last. "Perhaps if you have nothing better to do, you could help me hang them all out to dry."

But Willie the worm had popped back underground, and Sam the spider had scuttled away to find his hat.

Now Cordelia the centipede has ONE HUNDRED SOCKS... she seems to have muddled them up... can you help her to match FIFTY PAIRS?

Pippin Goes to School

One fine morning, around lunch time, Ma and Pa Bramley were passing the school playground with their pet pig, Pippin. All the children knew Pippin, and before Ma and Pa Bramley could stop her, their little pet pig had pushed open the gate and trotted into the yard.

"Look, Pippin has come to play with us," yelled a little girl.

"She's just in time for lunch!" cried the rest of the children. "Please can she stay?" they called to their teacher when she came out to ring the bell.

"What a lovely smell," chuckled Pippin as she wrinkled up her nose. "Cheese pie and chips with jelly and ice-cream to follow. That's my favourite!"

The teacher said that Pippin could stay at school the rest of the day if she liked. So off went Ma and Pa Bramley, smiling quietly to themselves.

That afternoon the children had a music lesson. Pippin shared a songbook with a little girl and sang all the verses at the top of her voice.

Then the children played instruments and Pippin, of course, joined in. She tried the triangle and the tambourine, but she liked the bongo drums best, because they made the most noise!

All too soon lessons were over and it was time to go home.

Pippin rushed outside with the rest of the children, and there Ma and Pa Bramley were waiting for her at the school gate.

"I like school so much," Pippin told them, "I shall come every day!"

Suddenly a boy carrying a pile of books came running up to Pippin.

"Pippin, you've forgotten all your homework!" he shouted.

Ma and Pa Bramley just smiled at each other and took Pippin home.

As soon as she had finished her tea, Pippin opened her books and began her homework.

It took her all night to do one page of sums. "Adding up and taking away is so hard!" yawned poor Pippin as she looked at the clock.

"I'm afraid it's getting very late, Pippin," whispered Ma Bramley, as she and Pa peeped round the door. "It's time we were all in bed."

"I quite agree with you," said young Pippin, letting out a sigh. "Tomorrow when I go to school, I think I'll just go for lunch!"

And that made Ma and Pa Bramley laugh out loud!

I don't think Pippin will make a very good student, do you?

The Birds' Town House

When Grandma Daisy was a little girl, she lived in the country. She loved all the different birds in the fields and trees around her cottage.

But when she grew older, she moved into town. "I'm really happy here in my little home," said Grandma Daisy, "but I do miss the country and the songs of so many birds."

Early one spring her grandson Ashley gave her a climbing plant.

"What is it called?" asked Grandma.

"Not sure, Grandma," Ashley replied with a grin. "I'm afraid I've lost the label. Just plant it and wait and see!"

So Grandma Daisy did just that. A few weeks went by. The days were warm and sunny and the plant began to grow. It grew so fast it was soon as high as Grandma Daisy's bedroom window... and it was still growing!

Early one bright morning, Grandma Daisy awoke to a very familiar sound.

She opened her bedroom window and popped her head out. Two blackbirds were building their nest in her new plant.

"How lovely!" said Grandma Daisy, clapping her hands in glee. "It's just like living in the country once more!"

Later that day she went to the shops and bought a bird-box and hung it up in the plant's branches.

Passers-by saw the box and the birds building their nests, so they brought all kinds of bird-boxes for Grandma Daisy to hang up.

"It's just like living in the country now!" smiled Grandma Daisy... and I think all the birds would agree.

The Rooftop Mystery of Loch Noddie

Little Red Mac and his friend Tam O'Tatie lived in a little cottage on the shores of Loch Noddie. Once a week, on market day, they went off to the nearest town to do their shopping.

Now the nearest town was over the hills and far away – so they were often gone from their little cottage for the whole day.

"What a fine morning!" said Little Red Mac to his friend.

"But I do believe I can hear the rumble of thunder," said Tam O'Tatie as he gazed across the loch. "I hope it's not going to rain and spoil our shopping trip."

In any case, they got in their car and off they went.

After a little while a gigantic head on a long neck slowly rose out of the loch... it was the monster!

"I'm so hungry my tummy is rumbling," the monster said. Then he spied the little cottage by the side of the loch, "Ah, breakfast!" he smiled.

And with that, the monster took a huge bite out of the roof, then another, and another... until it was all gone!

When Little Red Mac and Tam O'Tatie returned from shopping, they couldn't believe their eyes.

"Our whole roof has disappeared!" cried Tam.

"There must have been a terrific storm while we were away!" gasped Little Red Mac, looking very shocked.

"I was sure I heard the rumble of thunder this morning," said Tam... (but we know better, don't we?)

That night Little Red Mac and Tam O'Tatie pitched their tent on the shore and lit a bright fire.

"Tonight we'll sleep under the stars," said Tam, "but first I shall play you all the tunes I know on my bagpipes."

"That sounds wonderful," smiled Little Red Mac, for he loved music played on the bagpipes. "Tomorrow we'll get up early and repair our cottage roof. It won't take very long!"

Now someone we know isn't getting much sleep at all... the poor monster has a tummy ache!

"Next time I'm hungry, I shall just take a small bite," the monster groaned. "I will never ever eat a whole roof again. I was far too greedy!"

Helen's Black Eyes

Helen Hamster was very inquisitive. "I just need to know!" she would say as she poked her little pink nose into something else.

One day her cousin Harry decided to teach Helen a lesson!

Very early in the morning he called at Helen's house. "I'm going bird-watching in the woods today," he told her, "and I would like a hot drink before I set off," and he placed his bag on top of the table.

"You're more than welcome," smiled Helen, "tea, coffee or hot chocolate, you know where the kitchen is, go ahead and make whatever you like!"

Now cousin Harry knew quite well that Helen wanted him out of the way, so she could search through his bag on her own – and this is exactly what she did!

"Peanut butter sandwiches, packet of mixed nuts, apple, map and compass... and a pair of binoculars!" said Helen, as she turned everything out onto the table.

"I've never looked through a pair of binoculars before," giggled Helen as she pressed them tight to her eyes and took a good look around.

Then she spotted something tucked inside cousin Harry's bag.

"It's an envelope," Helen sniggered, "I simply must read what's inside!"

So the inquisitive little hamster opened up the envelope and read... "DON'T BE NOSY HELEN!"

At that very moment cousin Harry came out of the kitchen. "Just look at yourself in the mirror!" he laughed. "I put black paint on the ends of my binoculars, and now you have two lovely black eyes. Serves you right, you inquisitive little hamster!"

Poor Helen's face went bright red, and she rushed off into the kitchen to make Harry another hot drink, and to wash away that awful black paint.

The Undersea Scooter

"I wish we were that fast!" said the first little fish as he watched the dolphins skimming through the water.

"I would love to be able to dart and flit and flash through the sea," the second little fish sighed.

"Let's swim up to the surface and watch the jet skis whizzing through the waves," suggested the third little fish.

"You're all too slow to catch a cold!" joked Oz the octopus when he overheard the little fishes grumbling.

"Come to my workshop first thing tomorrow and I'll see what I can do."

Now, it's quite amazing what kind of rubbish is thrown into the ocean: wheels, tyres, even bicycles. Oz the octopus could find a use for them all.

Next day when the three little fishes went over to the workshop, Oz had a big surprise for them. He had been busy for hours, tinkering and banging and hammering with all the tools in his tool box... and being an octopus, Oz could use lots of tools at the same time!

The three little fishes gasped in amazement when they saw what clever Oz had made – an undersea scooter with

an outboard motor!

"How fast will it go?" asked the three little fishes, their mouths wide open.

"As fast as you like," laughed Oz as he pressed the starter button.

All at once the three little fishes jumped on the underwater scooter, and they were speeding across the bottom of the ocean.

"Thanks a lot, Oz!" they yelled as they sped away.

But Oz was too busy tinkering and banging and hammering his next creation to hear them!

Moving House

Mother Teddy said to Father Teddy one day, "We really need a bigger house. Big Brother and Big Sister could do with more space. The teddy twins want rooms of their own, and Baby Ted would love a garden!"

So Father Teddy went out and bought a new house straight away. It seemed perfect!

When the young teddies went to see their new home for the first time, it was a wet and stormy day. The wind was howling and dark clouds filled the sky. The rain was pouring down and the house looked cold and gloomy.

"It's very spooky," grumbled Big Brother.

"Do you think it's haunted?" whispered Big Sister.

"We hate it!" wailed the twins.

"I want to go home!" cried Baby.

During the next week or two, Mother Teddy and Father Teddy and their friends were very busy.

On one of the sunniest of days, the young teddies went back to see their new home once more. To their surprise the house had been painted from top to bottom and the garden was full of the most beautiful bright flowers.

"Welcome to your new home!" cried Mother Teddy as she ran to greet them.

"We love it now!" shouted the little teddies, and they all jumped for joy and ran inside.

Sam and the Giant Snails

It had been raining hard all morning, and everything was dripping wet.

"Just perfect for a stroll along the garden wall," said Sam to Sylvia Snail.

"I love damp days!" said Sylvia. "Misty, moist mornings and cloudy weather are simply perfect for us snails!"

"And slugs," called a voice from half-way up the wall.

"Slither up here and enjoy the view," shouted Sam.

Soon a whole family of slippery slugs came sliding towards Sam and Sylvia.

"Wet weather is the best weather!" sang the smaller slugs as they munched on their lunch of lettuce leaves.

"We always come up here when there's a thunderstorm coming," Sylvia Snail whispered.

"So when the rain begins to pour, we can watch all those GIANT SNAILS down below!" gasped Sam.

"They're not giant snails," sniggered the smallest slug. "It's just people with umbrellas!" And all the slugs laughed.

As for Sam and Sylvia... they felt extremely silly!

Iggy Frog's Fright

Iggy Frog was sailing his little yacht at the edge of the river. He looked very glum!

"Why don't you join me for a swim?" asked his friend, Silver Minnow. "Come on, the water's lovely!"

"Not likely," whispered Iggy. "I've just seen two horrible monsters near the bank. They've got great big goggly eyes and bright red webbed feet!"

"Are they your monsters?" asked Silver Minnow, and he pointed to two small children in goggles and flippers.

"Silly Iggy. I think you're the one with goggly eyes and webbed feet!" laughed Silver Minnow.

Cat on a Hat

Rosie had a ginger cat; she called him Gingerbread. Everywhere that Rosie went her cat went too. Rosie loved Gingerbread very much.

Just before Rosie's fifth birthday, her family and friends asked her what presents she would like.

"Now I have Gingerbread," smiled Rosie, "I don't need anything else. He is the best present of all."

When Rosie's next birthday came round, she was in for quite a surprise, as you can see.

She had lots of gifts, and Gingerbread was on every one – even her hat!

Scary Cat

This Hallowe'en,
Will you come as a bat?
Will you groan and moan?
Shake your bones, rat-tat-tat?
Will you ride on a broom?
Wear a witch's hat?
"Better still," said Rosie,
"I'll come as a cat!"
"Oh no!" mewed Gingerbread,
"Do I look like that?"

Fat Cat on a Mat

Rosie was learning to knit.

"I think you should try something simple to begin with," said Mum.

"I'll knit a mat for Gingerbread!" said Rosie, and she began straight away.

As soon as Rosie's mat was finished, she put it on the floor in front of the fire.

Gingerbread jumped off Dad's armchair and settled down on his new mat. "Purrfect!" he purred.

Next day, when Rosie saw Gingerbread fast asleep on his mat, she couldn't believe her eyes.

"You've grown too fat for your mat already," Rosie gasped, "it's far too small!"

I think Gingerbread is teasing poor Rosie, don't you?

Mrs Rabbit's Slippery Slide

Mrs Rabbit always took every one of the little grey rabbits with her when she went shopping. She needed them to help her carry all the food back... those hungry little bunnies ate so much!

Now the rabbits' warm and cosy burrow was deep underground. Although the young rabbits didn't mind climbing all those steps with empty baskets, when they came back with heavy loads of shopping, it was really hard to get back down the stairs without spilling some of it.

So one day while the family was away, Father Rabbit and a few of his friends solved the problem. When the bunnies came home, their baskets full of lovely things to eat, they were in for quite a surprise!

"It's our very own slippery slide!" they shouted all at once, then they whizzed from top to bottom in a flash.

Can you spot the loaves of crusty French bread they have brought back for Father Rabbit... I think he deserves it, don't you?

Squares, Stripes, Dots and Spots

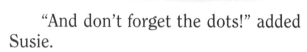

Steve liked stripes! Susie liked squares! Everything they had was stripes or squares, as you can see.

Then one day Steve said to Susie, "I'm fed up of stripes!"

"How very odd," said Susie to Steve, "I've had enough of squares. Whatever shall we do?"

At that very moment the family dog walked by.

"Spots!" cried Steve.

"And don't forget the dots!" added Susie.

So straight away they went out and bought everything they could find that was covered in spots or dots.

You can see how well it all matches, even the dog! But can you guess his name... is it Spot, or is it Dot?

Teddy Parks the Car

Teddy, the office bear, went to work every day in the city.

Now Teddy owned a very special car, which was small enough to park anywhere he wanted. It was very useful in such a busy place. Teddy called it his 'city car'.

One rainy morning, Teddy got up before it was light. "I shall go to the office very early today, then I will miss all those dreadful traffic jams!"

So Teddy set off in the dark and parked his little city car right in front of his office.

When the others came to work, they didn't even notice Teddy was already busy at his computer, because they had all rushed over to the window to take a look outside.

"Somebody has parked their car right in the middle of the fountain in front of our office building!" and everyone roared with laughter.

I wonder who it could be, Teddy, don't you?

Ashley's Messy Masterpiece

Ashley was always in a mess. "I think dirt finds you!" said his mother as she gazed at a large pile of his grubby clothes.

"Here is a clean white T-shirt!" she sighed, as she held up the third on that morning. "Try not to get it dirty!"

Now Ashley had a new hobby. He had just joined a painting class. Can you believe it? His mother couldn't either!

As it happened young Ashley was quite good at painting, although he was rather messy.

His teacher would marvel at his work – from a safe distance of course!

This particular morning, Ashley painted a wonderful picture.

"It's a masterpiece!" gasped his teacher from across the room.

"It just needs a blob of yellow," called Ashley, as he reached across the table for his paint.

Now because this was Ashley, he leaned a little too far and his painting stuck to the front of his T-shirt. Very

58

The Bouncing Baby

Jed always tried to set a good example for his baby sister.

"She will try to copy everything she sees you do!" said his mother.

So Jed tried very hard not to teach his baby sister bad habits.

Jed's sister has a new baby bouncer. She loves it, bouncing up and down!

Look at Jed bouncing on his bed. He loves it, bouncing up and down!

Should you be bouncing on your bed, Jed? Or is your baby sister setting you a bad example?

gently, Ashley peeled it off.

"Another masterpiece!" his teacher exclaimed as he ventured closer. "Sign it, we'll have it printed, then everyone can wear an Ashley T-shirt!"

When the T-shirt was printed and Ashley showed it to his mother, he grinned from ear to ear and said, "It's not a mess, it's a masterpiece!"

The Too Big Pyjamas

Abigail's auntie made her some new pyjamas, but when she measured the little girl, Abigail's cat kept playing with the tape measure.

Now when the pyjamas were finished and Abigail tried them on, they were far too big.

"My goodness!" gasped her auntie. "I must have gotten your measurements wrong. I can't imagine how I did that."

"I can!" said Abigail with a sigh, as she looked at her little cat.

So Abigail's auntie unpicked the pyjamas and made them all over again. This time they fitted perfectly and Abigail was delighted.

"Whatever am I going to do with all this material that's left over?" asked her auntie.

"Teddy could do with a pair of pyjamas," giggled Abigail.

"There'll still be plenty left over," said auntie.

"Then how about making some for my doll?" suggested Abigail.

"Does anyone else you know need a pair?" asked her aunt.

Then Abigail's cat, who had been sitting listening, jumped off the sofa and hid under the chair.

"Don't worry," chuckled Abigail. "There'll be no pyjamas for you!"

The Great Vegetable Race

Arabella Aubergine was taking a stroll along the garden path one bright morning when she spotted a large notice pinned to the fence.

"It's THE GREAT VEGETABLE SHOW next week," she gasped as she read the notice. "I'm so exotic and amazingly attractive, I'm sure to win first prize!"

So straight away she hurried back down the garden path to tell the other vegetables.

"Amazingly attractive Arabella Aubergine wins the silver cup for BEST VEGETABLE IN THE SHOW," Arabella smiled to herself and sighed, "I'm so wonderful, I'm bound to win!"

When the other vegetables heard

about the show they rushed down the garden to read the notice for themselves. They reached the fence puffing and panting and quite out of breath.

"That silly Arabella Aubergine!" grumbled a parsnip. "Can't she read?" he went on. "It says the silver cup will be presented to the fastest vegetable in the show. It's a race, not a beauty contest!"

"If it is a race," puffed Pip the potato, still out of breath, "we must all get fit as soon as possible. So let's start by doing press-ups. I'll show you how it's done!"

So Pip the potato got down on the grass and started straight away. After the first twenty press-ups poor Pip was quite out of breath. "I'll have to rest for a

minute," he wheezed, "I'm boiling!"

Now this made the young radishes scream with laughter until they turned redder than usual.

They began to dance around and jump up and down, singing at the tops of their squeaky little voices, "Boiled potatoes, mashed potatoes, baked potatoes, chips!" again and again and again.

The spring onions, who had been doing aerobics in the garden, heard all the noise and scampered across to join the radishes.

"Disco dancing is a great way to keep fit," called a tiny onion. "Come on everybody, join in!"

Soon all the vegetables were dancing and having a marvellous time.

Suddenly, one of the carrots noticed that the beans were missing. So he ran down the garden path to look for them.

There they were, laid out in the vegetable patch, dozing in the warm sun.

"You should be getting fit for the race at The Great Vegetable Show," cried the carrot, "not lazing in the sun!"

"No worries!" said the beans, who turned over and went to sleep.

All too soon the day of the race arrived. The vegetables lined up and Arabella Aubergine waved the flag to begin the race – she was far too grand to take part!

Everyone got off to a flying start. Pip the potato took the lead with the tomatoes close behind. The young radishes got the giggles and rolled all over the track, and the peas got so puffed... they popped!

Then all of a sudden the beans came striding by. Quick as a flash they passed the rest of the vegetables and were over the finishing line before you could blink.

"Well done!" gasped Pip the potato. "How did you win the race so easily without keeping fit?"

"Easy!" laughed the beans. "Have you forgotten? We're RUNNER BEANS!"

Dora the Snorer Makes a Move

Dora the snorer lived in a neat little house right on the edge of Whiskertown.

She lived at number three, the High Street, but you'll never have any problem finding Dora's house – just take a look at the neighbours!

Here are some of them leaving their houses... they are half-asleep and look very tired indeed. And it's all because of Dora... Dora the snorer the neighbours call her!

Every night she snores so loudly that no-one can get any sleep!

It so happened that Dora the dormouse had lots of country cousins. Several times a year she would pack her bags and go to stay with one of them.

It was the only time her poor neighbours got any peace.

While she was away enjoying the fresh air in the countryside, Dora saw the most wonderful cottage with a FOR SALE sign outside.

"Isn't it a dream?" she said to her cousin, Davy. "I could settle here for the rest of my life!"

Her cousin Davy looked a bit worried. "I think I should go out and check with the neighbours," he said, as he hurried off to find out who lived next door.

"Why on Earth should you do that?" said Dora, quite annoyed. "I get on extremely well with my neighbours in town!"

But cousin Davy knew all about Dora's snoring.

"What a stroke of luck!" cried Davy as he leaned over the cottage wall. "Your new neighbours are an owl, a family of bats and two rather shy hedgehogs."

"How lovely!" said Dora. "But why is that so lucky?"

"They're out all night and go to sleep during the day," muttered Davy, a bit embarrassed, "so they'll never hear you SNORING!"

"I do snore rather loudly!" grinned Dora, as she scampered off to buy her dream cottage.

The Apple Peel Contest

Mrs Hedgehog was busy baking. She was well known in Woodland for her scrumptious apple pies. So, as kind Mr Grey Badger had brought her a huge box of apples, she decided to invite all her neighbours round for an apple pie supper that night.

"Why do we need so many apple pies?" asked Baby Hedgehog.

"Because," said his mother, "folks don't eat just one slice, they eat two or three and sometimes four. In fact, I have known Mr Grey Badger to eat a whole apple pie with a jug full of fresh cream poured on top!"

"You'd better get busy then," Baby Hedgehog told his mother.

"I thought all of you young ones could lend a hand," smiled Mrs Hedgehog. "Do you think that you could manage to peel and slice the apples for me?"

The little hedgehogs groaned. "We all hate peeling apples," they chorused. "We want to go out to play!"

"Then I'll make it into a game," suggested Mrs Hedgehog. "I'll give a prize to the one who can cut off the most apple peel in one piece." And Mrs Hedgehog showed them how. "If you're very careful it can be done," and she held up a long curly length of peel.

"Whoever has the longest piece of apple peel will be the winner!" and she bustled off to make her pastry.

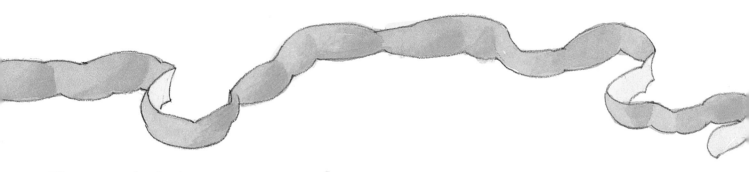

The young hedgehogs thought this sounded like fun, so they each sat down with a bowl of apples and a little peeler.

They were all a bit clumsy at first. They hacked away at the apples and chunks of fruit, with the peel flying in all directions.

Now Baby Hedgehog left the others and went to sit in a corner to practise his peeling. Very soon he could peel a whole apple in one go!

As he worked away quietly, he didn't notice that a family of hungry caterpillars had wriggled across the grass and were munching their way through the apple peel.

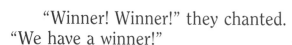

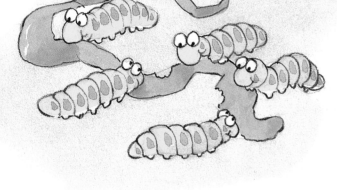

"Winner! Winner!" they chanted. "We have a winner!"

At supper that evening everyone ate lots and lots of apple pie. And Mrs Hedgehog baked a special one... just for Baby Hedgehog and the caterpillars!

They munched and crunched so quickly that when Baby Hedgehog looked down, there wasn't a trace of peel left.

"Sorry!" said the caterpillars as they swallowed one last mouthful. "We were very hungry and your apple peel looked so tempting!"

In a while all the other young hedgehogs gathered round and watched Baby Hedgehog peel his last apple in one go.

What Ugly Mugs!

Have you ever wondered what happens when you put away the cups and saucers and plates and mugs at the end of the day, when you close the kitchen cupboard, switch off the light and go to bed for the night?

Lots more happens than you would ever imagine. Let's listen and find out...

"The mugs in this cupboard are getting totally out of hand!" said the coffeepot, looking very serious. The teapot nodded. "They're rude and cheeky and sometimes they fight. Most of them are chipped and one or two of the bigger ones are cracked!"

The coffeepot shook his head. "I think we are to blame, teapot! The mugs are simply copying our bad behaviour."

"I know what you mean," the teapot agreed. "We spend all our time arguing and shouting and letting off steam!"

"We're always bad tempered and full of hot air," the coffeepot sighed, "but we don't really mean the nasty things we say to each other, do we?"

The teapot smiled, "Goodness me, no! It's just a bit of fun between the two of us. We're just letting off steam!"

So there and then, the coffeepot and teapot settled down to try to find a way to make the mugs in the cupboard behave themselves.

After lots of strong tea and hot coffee, they came up with an idea.

"Can you remember those dainty china teacups packed in tissue paper on the bottom shelf?" asked the teapot.

"I know the ones!" said the coffeepot. "They're so pretty and delicate, they only come out on very special occasions."

"Let's ask them to join us and meet the mugs," suggested the teapot.

"I hope you know what you're doing!" said the coffeepot, wincing.

When the pretty china teacups came visiting the next evening, the mugs were already in the middle of a fight.

"You bunch of ugly mugs!" the biggest mug was yelling at the top of his voice.

One of the tiny teacups was so surprised at such bad behaviour, she fell over backwards. Quick as a flash, the big mug leapt off the shelf and saved her.

"My hero!" the tiny teacup cried in a tinkly little voice. "You've saved me from being smashed into a thousand pieces!" and she gave the big mug the softest of kisses.

Now you can believe it, from that moment on, all the mugs behaved perfectly. No more fighting or being rude to one another. Instead they became polite and well-mannered.

The dainty little teacups showed the big mugs how to waltz and do the rhumba, they even taught the spoons to line dance.

"Great idea of mine!" said the coffeepot.

"I thought it was my idea," remarked the teapot, "but let's not argue about it!"

Come Under My Umbrella

Beverly had a very special doll, called Rainbow. She was dressed in a waterproof coat and a rainhat, and she was holding an umbrella. Rainbow was Beverly's favourite doll!

One or two of the other dolls teased poor Rainbow.

"Why do you need that silly umbrella when we are always indoors?" they jeered.

"Pay no attention to them," said a friendly teddy bear. "Your umbrella will come in useful one day, I'm sure!"

And so it did...

It was a very hot summer's afternoon, and Beverly changed into her shorts and T-shirt and went to play at her friend's house, but she forgot to close her bedroom window.

The toys were pleased, for they were sitting in a row on the window seat, and the breeze that blew gently through the open window felt cool and refreshing.

All of a sudden the sky outside grew dark, lightning flashed, thunder rumbled and then the rain lashed down. It poured and poured through the open window onto the toys below.

"Quick, come under my umbrella," cried Rainbow; "or your clothes and hair will be ruined!"

The dolls who had teased Rainbow looked very ashamed as they squeezed under the umbrella.

"I told you it would come in useful one day!" smiled the teddy bear with a wink.

Atishoo, a Tissue

Mr Magic had a little white rabbit called Snowdrop, who helped him with his tricks.

Now Mr Magic had a bad cold and had to stay in his bedroom all day. Snowdrop could hear him sneezing as he scampered up the stairs.

"Atishoo! Atishoo!" Mr Magic sneezed loudly. "A tissue, a tissue, please pass me a tissue!"

So Snowdrop hurried into Mr Magic's bedroom and began to search for a box of tissues.

Now Mr Magic's bedroom was full of boxes that he used in his magic shows. And in the very last box, after making quite a mess, Snowdrop found the tissues. Atishoo! Atishoo!

Paws, Claws and Jaws

At the end of term a photographer came to school to take pictures of all the children.

He was about to pack away his lights and cameras when Mrs Bloomer, the teacher, shouted to him. "There are three more photos to take before you go!"

"Have I missed someone?" the photographer asked.

"Indeed you have!" said Mrs Bloomer. "You must photograph Paws, Claws and Jaws before you go!"

The photographer looked very worried, until he saw who Paws, Claws and Jaws were!

The Speedy Little Tractor

One spring Farmer Bonnett ordered a new tractor to work on his farm.

"I hope it's powerful and very fast!" said his son Jake.

"It's just a little tractor for smaller jobs," the farmer's wife said with a smile. "It will be perfect for me to drive," and off she went to feed the chickens.

"Oh great," muttered Jake. "We're buying a new tractor just big enough for my mum to drive," and he stuck both hands in his pockets and ambled off towards the tractor shed.

Now Jake loved driving, and although he enjoyed driving the trucks and tractors around the farm, he really wanted to be a racing driver.

When the new tractor arrived, it was bright and shiny but very, very small.

"Isn't it dainty?" gasped the farmer's wife as she hopped up onto the seat and tootled off slowly round the farmyard.

"Our new little tractor ought to have a name," she cooed. "I think I'll call her Trisha! Trisha the tractor!"

Next day it was perfect weather for ploughing. So Farmer Bonnett asked Jake to drive the new tractor down the lane, over the hill and into the top field.

"Must I?" moaned Jake. "Have I got to drive a silly little tractor called Trisha?"

But all the same, he knew the top field needed ploughing.

Jake started up the little tractor, but before he could settle back in his seat Trisha had roared across the farmyard, raced down the lane, shot up the hill at top speed and had come to a halt at the field gate!

"Never mind the ploughing," cried Jake in delight, "let's see how you can really move!"

All that morning Jake raced with the little tractor across fields, down lanes and along the main road. They whizzed past every vehicle in sight, even the fastest sports cars.

When Farmer Bonnett heard all about Trisha the tractor, he thought for a minute. "I've got an idea. You always wanted to be a racing driver, Jake. Why don't I do the ploughing while you get Trisha ready for the Racing Grand Prix next weekend?"

"Oh yeah, Dad!" exclaimed Jake.

"That would be great."

When the day of the race finally arrived, all the powerful racing cars lined up side by side on the grid with the little tractor in the middle. The farmer's wife had put stickers on Jake's boiler suit and helmet, so he looked just like all the other racing drivers.

All the cars sniggered at Trisha and giggled behind her back; even the crowd looked puzzled. Who ever heard of a tractor racing in a Grand Prix?

The race began, and the cars whizzed

round the circuit. Trisha was faster than any of them and was soon in front.

All the racing cars had to stop in the pits, but not Trisha, she just kept going at top speed and won the race in record time – six laps ahead!

After the race had finished one of the mechanics asked Jake if he could look under Trisha's bonnet.

Was he in for a surprise! Lo and behold, he found that Trisha had been fitted with a racing car engine by mistake at the factory, and didn't have a tractor engine at all!

How Farmer Bonnett and his wife laughed. "Well, at least I shall get my ploughing done in double quick time!"

As for the poor drivers who lost the race, they didn't have time to laugh, they were too busy looking under their car bonnets... to see if they had a tractor engine by mistake!

The Squeaking Postman

Postman Plumtree got up early every morning except on a Sunday. He set his alarm for four-thirty, and by five o'clock he had finished his breakfast and was getting into his van ready to deliver the mail.

Now one morning, Postman Plumtree jumped into his post van as usual, and it simply wouldn't start!

"Oh dear!" said Postman Plumtree. "This will never do! I shall have to ring the garage and speak to the mechanic."

"Do you know it's five o'clock in the morning?" yawned Matt the mechanic.

But because he knew that it was an emergency, Matt got out of bed at once and drove over to look at Postman Plumtree's van. If anybody would be able to fix the van, it would be Matt. He was the best mechanic in town!

Matt opened the bonnet and shook his head. "Serious stuff, Postman Plumtree! I'll have to tow your van back to the garage and take a look. Can't even promise when that will be!" he shouted as he towed the van away. "I'm very, very busy at the moment!"

So straight away Postman Plumtree went to his shed and took out his old bike.

"Couldn't have happened on a worse day," muttered Postman Plumtree, "there are phone bills and gas bills and water bills and electricity bills to deliver to every single house!"

So Postman Plumtree, who by now was running very late, jumped on his old bike and peddled furiously into town, whistling all the way.

He whistled so loudly, he didn't even notice his old bike making the most dreadful squeaking noise. You could hear it all over town.

People ran out of their houses, grabbed their letters and rushed back inside, slamming their doors shut tight to get away from that dreadful squeaking.

"Folks are being really helpful this morning," grinned Postman Plumtree, "they're all running out and picking up their mail. They must have realized that my van has broken down." Then he went on his way, whistling loudly with his old bike still making that dreadful squeaking noise.

Postman Plumtree finished his
round in next to no time, but before he
went off fishing for the rest of the day,
he telephoned Matt the mechanic.

"There's no rush at all with my post
van," he said. "I think I'll use my old
bike for a while. I deliver the letters
much quicker!"

Mr Munro's Moustache

Mr Munro was very well-mannered. He raised his hat to everyone he met and smiled politely. But Mr Munro never said a word, because he was so shy...

So the next afternoon, shy Mr Munro put on a false moustache, pulled his hat well down over his head, and went to the tea shop. When he arrived, he peered round the door and spotted a quiet table in the corner.

Until one day, when he met the girl of his dreams!

She was quiet and charming, with a ribbon in her hair, and she owned a tea shop in the town square.

"I'm far too shy to speak to the girl of my dreams," sighed Mr Munro, "so I shall visit her tea shop in disguise!"

When the girl of his dreams had served Mr Munro tea and cakes, she hid behind her tray.

"Perhaps the girl of my dreams is as shy as me," thought Mr Munro, and he took a big bite of his cake.

All of a sudden, the girl of his dreams dropped her tray with a loud crash!

"Thank goodness!" she cried. "I thought you were a burglar waiting to rob my tea shop!"

And when Mr Munro looked at his cake, there was his moustache stuck to the icing! So Mr Munro and the girl of his dreams sat down at the table and had tea together. They talked and laughed and neither of them felt the least bit shy.

"What a clever disguise," said the girl of his dreams, and as she passed Mr Munro another cake... she fluttered her eyelashes!

The Balloon Circus

It was the day of the school party. All morning the children helped their teachers blow up balloons and decorate the school hall with streamers and flags.

In the afternoon someone came along to show the children how to do face painting. The teachers had their faces painted first, which made all the children laugh.

The twins had their faces painted quite differently.

"Now we don't look a bit alike!" giggled one twin.

When the party ended and the time came to go home, the head teacher looked around the school hall and shook his head.

"We seem to have blown up far too many balloons this year. So take as many home as you can manage, children!"

So the twins arrived back at their house with painted faces and a huge bunch of balloons in each hand.

"Whatever are you going to do with all those balloons?" asked Dad as they floated around the room.

"Let's paint a face on every one!" suggested one of the twins.

"We'll make each one look different!" said the other.

So they took out their coloured pens and got busy.

"They look just like a collection of clowns!" said Dad when he came into the room and saw the balloons floating all over the place.

"I wish we could keep hold of them!" cried the twins as they jumped up and down trying to reach the balloons.

"When I was young," smiled Dad, "we made tiny feet out of card to stop the balloons from flying up to the ceiling!" And he showed them how to do it.

"What a great idea," said one of the twins, "our balloons look as if they have shoes on!"

That night, when the twins went to bed, they left their balloons on the table.

"They'll stay there until morning," Dad told them as he switched off the light.

But the balloons had other ideas! That night they put on their very own circus... but they made quite sure that they covered up Dad's prize cactus first!

Little Biddy Mouse Goes Out For Tea

Little Biddy Mouse was the youngest mouse in the family, in fact, he was just a baby! Although he was still very young and extremely small, it didn't stop him from getting into all sorts of mischief!

The older mice loved Little Biddy Mouse. They couldn't resist his great big smile and his cute little button nose. Both his grandmothers and all his aunts spoiled him terribly. But on one subject they were all as serious as could be!

"Never, ever, ever go outside the mouse-hole," they said, frowning, "you could be eaten by the cat, and if anyone sees you, especially ladies – they will scream and chase you out of the house, and we may never see you again!"

When they said this some of the aunts began to sniff and snuffle and blow their noses hard... it was the thought of never ever seeing Little Biddy Mouse again if he went outside the mouse-hole.

Now Little Biddy Mouse hadn't listened to a word. He'd been far too busy smiling his charming smile and wrinkling up his cute button nose.

So the very next time he was exploring near the mouse-hole, he popped his head outside and the rest of him followed.

"What a great place!" Little Biddy Mouse grinned. Then he wrinkled up his cute little button nose and sniffed the air. "And what wonderful smells!" He scampered off to investigate.

There, on a coffee table, not too high off the floor, were plates and dishes full of

scrumptious yummy cakes. So Little Biddy Mouse climbed up the lacy cloth that hung over the edge of the coffee table.

"Whatever shall I try first?" Little Biddy Mouse chuckled to himself, gazing at the tempting tea. "I'll try a little bit of everything!" So he picked up a tiny silver spoon and began straight away.

All of a sudden, one lady who was helping herself to a chocolate eclair

spotted Little Biddy Mouse, and let out a blood-curdling scream!

Little Biddy Mouse gave her his biggest smile and wrinkled up his cute little button nose.

When the other ladies saw him, they screamed too. But Little Biddy Mouse just kept on smiling in the most charming way. That was too much for the ladies. Instead of chasing Little Biddy Mouse, they ran shrieking and screaming from the room.

"I thought I was supposed to run away, not them!" he cried.

Little Biddy Mouse packed up some of the lovely food from the coffee table and took it back through the mouse-hole.

When Little Biddy Mouse told of his adventures, some of the aunts were so shocked, they fainted. So Little Biddy Mouse gave them a taste of the chocolate gateau he had brought back, which made them feel much better.

"You see, everyone, I didn't get chased at all and I'm safe home again!" said Little Biddy Mouse, wrinkling up his little button nose and giving everyone a great big smile!

Baby Rabbit's Winter Garden

It was a dark and dismal winter's day with frost on the ground and a bitter wind howling through the woods.

The youngest grey rabbit had a very bad cold.

"I've never had a cold before!" sniffed Baby Rabbit. "My nose is running, my eyes are sore and I can't stop sneezing. I don't like having a cold. I wish it would go away!"

"I think you're feeling sorry for yourself," his mother smiled. "And I do believe you're bored!"

All the other young rabbits were at school, and Baby Rabbit had no-one to play with until they came home.

"How long do colds last?"
Baby Rabbit sniffed and snuffled.

"A bad cold can last up to a
week, sometimes longer!" replied
Mrs Rabbit.

"I don't believe it!" cried Baby
Rabbit, starting to sneeze. "Now
I really do feel sorry for myself.
Atishoo! Atishoo!"

"I know how to cheer you up,"
chuckled his mother, "you can help
me do a spot of gardening."

Baby Rabbit groaned, "I hate
gardening! It's winter and it's far
too cold to go outside."

"Just teasing!" laughed Mrs
Rabbit. "We'll do some indoor
gardening instead."

So she went to her special
cupboard where she kept all kinds
of things to make on rainy days
and to amuse bored bunnies.

Out of a box in her cupboard
she took a packet of seeds and the
strangest pottery animals Baby
Rabbit had ever seen.

"Are they money boxes?" he
asked.

"Goodness me, no!" laughed his mother. "In these special pots we are going to plant a cress garden."

"I love cress sandwiches," cried Baby Rabbit. "They're my favourite!"

So they put some cotton wool into the special pots, then moistened it with water and sprinkled on the tiny seeds.

"Remember to water them every day," whispered Mrs Rabbit, "and try to keep our cress gardens a secret!"

The cress grew very quickly. In a few days it was ready for cutting, and Baby Rabbit's cold was completely better.

He couldn't wait to tell the others about his indoor gardening. When the other little rabbits were shown the special pots of cress they were delighted. They all helped to make cress and mayonnaise sandwiches and ate them for tea.

"I want to sow some more seeds straight away!" cried Baby Rabbit. "Those sandwiches were delicious!"

91

Good Night, Moon!
Sleep Tight!

The moon and the stars looked down from the sky. The whole world below was fast asleep.

"It makes me feel so tired when I can see that everybody except me is tucked up in bed!" said the moon, giving a gigantic YAWN!

"Please don't do that again!" shrieked the stars as they tumbled and tossed all over the sky.

But the poor moon was so dreadfully tired he just kept on yawning.

"You can't go to sleep until daylight," said a tiny star as he somersaulted past. "Not everybody down there is asleep. If someone below looks up and sees that you've nodded off - we'll all be in trouble!"

Just then a small cloud floated gently by.

"Grab onto that cloud!" cried a star, who was much brighter than the rest.

So the stars got together and pushed the small cloud in front of the tired moon.

"Now you can go to sleep," the stars twinkled as they laughed. "The whole world below will think that the moon has just gone behind a cloud!"

I see the moon,
And the moon sees me.
God bless the moon,
And God bless me.